powerful man in the universe and the protector of Castle Grayskull. Prince Adam's pet tiger Cringer turned into the mighty Battle Cat, He-Man's faithful companion.

Only Orko, the court magician, and Man-at-Arms, He-Man's best friend, knew this secret. Even Prince Adam's parents and Teela, captain of the guard, saw him only as the prince of Eternia. Prince Adam kept his secret because danger lived on Eternia.

On one side of the planet, the sun never shined. There, inside Snake Mountain, the wicked Skeletor planned new ways to find

out Castle Grayskull's secrets. And still others with bad intentions waited on other worlds, ready to disturb Eternia's peaceful way of life.

Against them all stood only He-Man and the Masters of the Universe!

SKELETOR'S
FLOWER OF POWER

Written by Bryce Knorr

Illustrated by Harry J. Quinn and James Holloway

Creative Direction by Jacquelyn A. Lloyd

Design Direction by Ralph E. Eckerstrom

A GOLDEN BOOK

Western Publishing Company, Inc.
Racine, Wisconsin 53404

Library of Congress Catalog Card Number 84-62344
ISBN 0-932631-01-0
A B C D E F G H I J

Classic™ Binding U.S. Patent #4,408,780
Patented in Canada 1984.
Patents in other countries issued or pending.
R. R. Donnelley and Sons Company

"A sword can be your friend, Prince Adam," Man-at-Arms said. "But what if you don't have one? Fisto will show you what to do."

"My hands are all I need," Fisto said. "Get ready, Prince Adam." Fisto moved with great speed. He took Prince Adam's arm and yanked hard. The prince sailed through the air and landed on the soft practice mat.

"I'm glad this was only practice, Fisto," Prince Adam said. He shook Fisto's hand—carefully.

"Don't worry," Fisto laughed. "Your lesson is over. It's important to remember, though, that whatever the weapon, we must use it only in self defense. Even our hands."

"That is today's most important lesson," Man-at-Arms said. "We fight only if there is no other way to protect ourselves."

Orko floated by the gym door. He watched Prince Adam's class.

"I want to be a fighter, too," Orko said. "I'll show Man-at-Arms I know how. My magic will help me sneak inside."

Orko disappeared in a puff. Inside the gym, a blaster moved all by itself.

Suddenly, a blue ray ripped the room. Orko appeared, holding the blaster. He looked very surprised—and very scared!

"How do I turn it off?" Orko yelled.

Prince Adam remembered Fisto's teaching. The prince knocked the blaster away from Orko.

"You learn quickly, Prince Adam," Man-at-Arms said. "But Orko, I wish you would learn. You are not a fighter. You are a magician."

"What is this blaster?" Prince Adam asked.
"It didn't blow things up. It broke them."

"It's my new freeze-blaster," said Man-at-Arms. "It shoots a ray of cold. I…"

The ground around them suddenly shook.

"That was no freeze-blaster!" said Man-at-Arms. "Come, Fisto. Let's see what it is. Prince Adam, make sure Orko cleans up his mess."

Prince Adam drew his Power Sword.

"I wish He-Man could help you," Prince Adam said. **"But he's needed outside. And Orko, Man-at-Arms is right. You are good at magic. You don't need to be a fighter."**

He raised the Power Sword.

"By the power of Grayskull. I HAVE THE POWER!"

He-Man ran out of the palace. His friends were chasing a strange animal. "Yeeeeep," it yelled and bounced about on its stomach.

"Don't fire!" He-Man said. **"The poor animal is only scared."**

The animal hopped over the palace wall with a loud "yeeeeep!"

"Follow him, Buzz-Off," He-Man told his flying scout.
"I must make sure everyone is safe. I'll catch up with you."

No one was hurt. He-Man jumped on Stridor and found Buzz-Off. The scout was puzzled.

"The beast disappeared," Buzz-Off said. "Right into thin air!"

Orko sat sadly in the gym.

"Prince Adam is right," Orko said. "I'm a magician. I'll use my magic. I'll find something everyone will like."

Orko walked away from the palace. He was thinking very hard. He didn't see Skeletor hiding behind a rock.

"**Orko is just what I need,**" Skeletor thought. He changed into an old man.

"**Perhaps, wise magician, I can help you,**" the old man said. He stepped from behind the rock.

"**I give you this flower. It grows only in a far-off land. It has magic powers. Anyone near it feels happy.**"

Orko smelled the flower. He fastened it to his hat. Right away he felt better!

"It works!" Orko said. "I wish I had lots of them. Everyone would be happy."

"I have only one of them," the man said.

"But your magic can make as many as you want."

Orko said a spell and floated back toward the palace. Soon, he had many, many flowers.

"I'll give them to everyone!" he said.

When Orko left, the man let out a laugh. With a wave of his hand he became Skeletor.

"Orko took my bait," he said.
"It's just as I planned. With these remote-control flowers, I can make people do what I want. Soon, Eternia will be mine!"

Orko's flowers soon were found everywhere. They were Eternia's newest fad.

"Aren't they pretty, Father?" Teela asked Man-at-Arms.

"Yes, they are, Teela," he said. "I feel better when I'm around them."

Everyone loved the flowers. Everyone except Prince Adam.
"Ah-choo!" he sneezed.
"I must be allergic to them.
"The others seem happy. But the look on their faces is so faraway. It's almost as if someone is talking to them."
Prince Adam held his nose. He put a flower into a metal box.

"First, a strange brown animal appears in the palace courtyard. And now Orko's brown flowers are having an odd effect on people. Something may be very, very wrong. I need help with this mystery."

Prince Adam pulled out his Power Sword.

"By the power of Grayskull...

"I HAVE THE POWER!"

"Be happy—what a bad idea," Skeletor said.
"My thought machine should give new orders through the flowers. Orders to make me king of Eternia!"

He turned the dials of a strange machine.

"Obey Skeletor! Ruler of all Eternia!" Skeletor yelled into the machine.

"Clawful! Jitsu! Let's visit my new palace! No one will stop me now!"

He-Man took the box containing one of the brown flowers to Castle Grayskull.

"You must solve this mystery, He-Man," said Sorceress. "Eternia is in great danger!"

"How can I find out more about this flower?" He-Man asked.

"Moss Man can help you," she said. "He has special powers over plants."

"Moss Man?" He-Man asked.
"I thought he was only a legend. Where does he live?"

"Go to the Evergreen Forest," Sorceress told him. "But *you* will not find Moss Man. *He* will find you. No eyes see Moss Man walk through the forest. He can hide anywhere."

He-Man flew Wind Raider far across Eternia. Deep in a green blanket of trees, he found a clearing.

No one else would have seen anything. But He-Man knew that other eyes watched him.

"Greetings, forest people," he said.
"He-Man comes in the name of good."

The trees and plants came to life. Strange green creatures stood all around He-Man. One stepped out and spoke.

"Even deep in the forest we know of He-Man's bravery," he said. "Why do you honor us with a visit?"

"Thank you, Moss Man," He-Man said. **"Eternia needs your help."**

He-Man gave the metal box to Moss Man.

"This looks like a flower," Moss Man said. "But it is a machine. I do not think it is from Eternia."

Zoar flew over the clearing. Sorceress, in falcon form, spoke.

"The flower must be from another dimension," she said.

"How did it get here?" He-Man asked.

"There must be a tunnel between the two worlds," Sorceress said.

"Of course!" He-Man said.
"That's why Buzz-Off saw the brown animal disappear. But who opened the tunnel?"

"To find out, see where the tunnel goes," she said.

He-Man and Moss Man got on Wind Raider. They showed Zoar where the animal disappeared.

"I will try to open the tunnel to the other dimension," Sorceress said.

Zoar's wings beat quickly.

"HURRY!" she said. "The tunnel is open."

He-Man and Moss man flew into the tunnel. 'Round and 'round and deeper and deeper they fell.

Finally, Wind Raider broke into the other world. A loud bang rang through the sky.

He-Man landed Wind Raider at the base of a big rock. White-topped mountains towered over them. He-Man sniffed danger in the cold air.

A band of fighters jumped down on them from the rock cliffs.
"We come in peace!" He-Man said.
"We won't hurt you. We need your help."
But the fighters moved in closer.
"We may have to fight back, Moss Man," He-Man said.

The sound of a loud "Yeeeeep!" stopped the battle.

"It's the same brown animal from the palace," He-Man said.

"He's not alone," Moss Man said. "Look at all his friends!"

The animals bounced to a stop and "Yeeeeeped" loudly. One of the men stepped forward and bowed.

"We are sorry," he said. "This is Sor-El, King of the Bronzaurs. He says you are his friend. So, we are your friends, too."

Sor-El nodded his brown, hairy head. He-Man could not help but smile back.

"I am A-Zor, of the Serulans," the man said. "How may we help you?"

He-Man opened the metal box.

The Serulans pulled out their swords.

"You come for the flowers, too," A-Zor yelled. "Just like the other one, Skeletor!"

"No!" He-Man said. **"He is my enemy."**

He-Man told them what happened. A-Zor agreed to help. He led them into the valley. The flowers were   all over. But the people were not happy. They were slaves!

"The flowers are not flowers," A-Zor said. "They are part of the thought machine."

"With Skeletor's help, the wicked Ver-Dant uses the machine to make these people obey him," A-Zor continued. "But it will not work in our own land. It is too cold."

"If Skeletor has a thought machine, Eternia is in trouble," He-Man said.

"We must go, A-Zor, but we'll be back. Thanks!"

"Bow before Skeletor, king of Eternia," Clawful said back at the palace. He shook his mighty hand.

King Randor was helpless. Skeletor's machine made the guards obey.

"No one can stop me now!" Skeletor said. ***"Not even He-Man! I rule Eternia!"***

But He-Man had a different idea.

"We know how to stop you, Skeletor," he said.

"Do you, He-Man?" Skeletor asked. ***"Your puny powers are no match for me now. I will watch your friends finish you forever.***

"Skeletor orders you to attack He-man!"

He-Man's friends moved like robots.

"I'll cover you, Moss Man," He-Man said. **"Start firing the freeze blaster."**

"I never met a flower I didn't like," Moss Man said. "Until now."

The ray froze the flowers. Skeletor's hold over He-Man's friends was broken.

"I'll get that blaster!" Jitsu said. He kicked the ray from Moss Man's hands. Then Clawful jumped at He-Man.

Orko woke up from the flower's power.

"My friends are in trouble," Orko thought. "I must help He-Man. That freeze blaster give me an idea."

He moved his hands quickly. Orko's magic made a pitcher of water. He poured the water on the floor. Then Orko picked up the blaster and fired.

"Watch out for the ice!" Skeletor cried. But it was too late. Jitsu and Clawful fell on the slippery floor.

He-Man and his friends surrounded Skeletor's men. The fight was over.

"You win this time, He-Man," Skeletor said. *"But some day I will rule Eternia!"*

Skeletor and his men disappeared.

"We gave Skeletor the slip, didn't we, He-Man?" Orko said.

"Speaking of slip," He-Man said.

"Let Man-at-Arms slip that blaster back where it belongs."

"Are you mad at me?" asked Orko.

"No, no," He-Man laughed.

"But next time, don't take gifts from strangers."

"Remember, fads can be fun. But like those flowers, they can also be trouble."

Moss Man was ready to go home. "Let's grow Skeletor some trouble, first," he said.

He-Man, with Orko and Moss Man along, flew Wind Raider over Snake Mountain.

"Anytime you're ready, Moss Man," He-Man said.

Moss Man pointed at Skeletor's castle. Right away, weeds grew wildly. In seconds, they covered Snake Mountain completely.

Skeletor ordered his men to cut down the plants. But they just ran away.

"Skeletor could use this freeze blaster," Orko said. "But he shouldn't take gifts from strangers, either."

"**That's right,**" He-Man said.
"**I have a much better use for it.**"

He-Man and Orko took Moss Man home. Then Zoar joined them in the sky.

"**Can you open the dimension tunnel, Sorceress?**" He-Man asked.

"It is done," Sorceress said.

A-Zor was glad to see them this time.

"This freeze blaster will help defeat Ver-Dant," He-Man said. **"Good luck."**

He-man and Orko got back into Wind Raider. Orko sneezed loudly.

"Are you allergic to me?" He-Man asked.

"No," Orko said. "That freeze blaster gave me a cold. But don't worry. That's one gift I won't give to anyone else."

THE END